Nikki Slade Robinson

Anywhere Artist

CLARION BOOKS
HOUGHTON MIFFLIN HARCOURT
BOSTON   NEW YORK

I am an anywhere artist.

I don't need paint or paper.

I can make art anywhere.

My imagination is all I need.

I am a forest artist.

I find fluffy lichen,
twisted sticks,
and smooth stones.
I pick up lacy leaf skeletons.

I can make **anything** I want!

I am a beach artist.

I collect salty shells.

I shape sand.

I spread curly seaweed out.

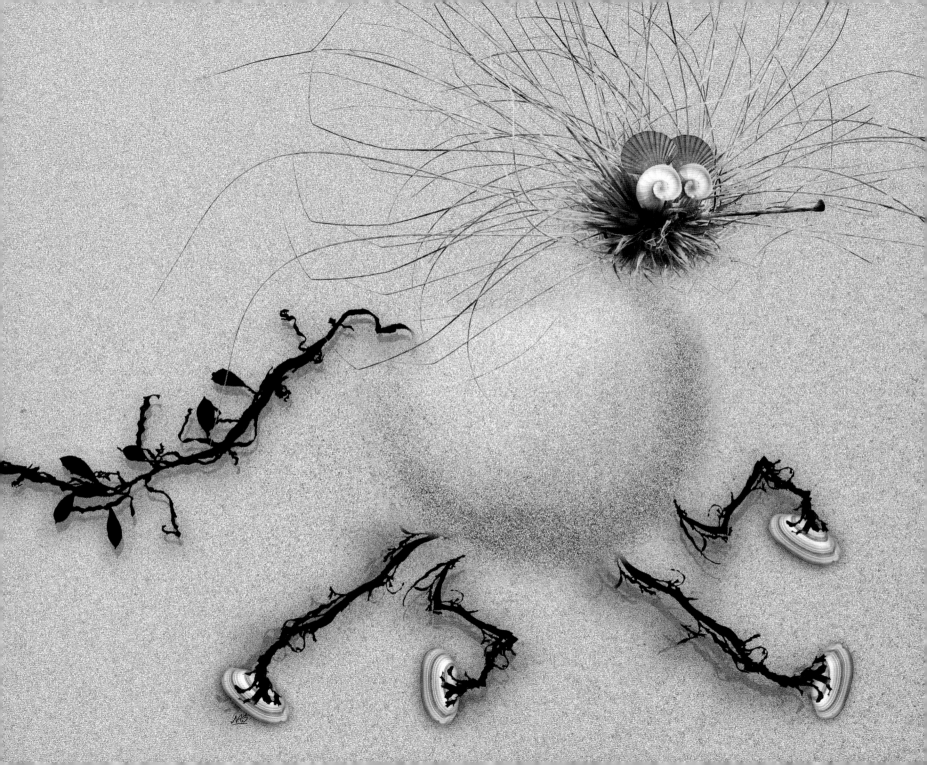

I use driftwood,

making it stand tall

to cast long-fingered shadows

over my art.

I am a rain artist.

My feet dance ringlet patterns in the puddles.

I squish OOzy mud

into Silly shapes.

I am a **sky** artist.

I lie on the grass
and make art inside my head.
The clouds are my paints.

My imagination is my brush.

Sometimes my art fills the WHOLE sky!

I can make art anywhere.
I can make art with anything.
I bet you can too!
So, what will you make today?

Clarion Books
3 Park Avenue
New York, New York 10016

Copyright © 2016 by Nikki Slade Robinson

First published in New Zealand in 2016 by Duck Creek Press,
an imprint of David Ling Publishing Ltd.
First US edition, 2018

Clarion Books is an imprint of Houghton Mifflin Harcourt Publishing Company.

www.hmhco.com

Library of Congress Cataloging-in-Publication Data is available.
ISBN 978-1-328-70736-9

Manufactured in China
SCP 10 9 8 7 6 5 4 3 2 1
4500686783